LINDSAY BARRETT GEORGE

Alfred Digs

GREENWILLOW BOOKS
An Imprint of HarperCollinsPublishers

For Paul, Steve, and Tim

Alfred Digs ————————————————————————————

Copyright © 2008 by Lindsay Barrett George
All rights reserved. Manufactured in China.
www.harpercollinschildrens.com

Watercolors and ink were used to prepare the full-color art.
The text type is Baskerville.

Library of Congress Cataloging-in-Publication Data
George, Lindsay Barrett. Alfred digs / by Lindsay Barrett George.
  p. cm.
"Greenwillow Books."
Summary: Alfred the aardvark lives with his mother on the "A"
page of the dictionary, and when his pet ant, Itty Bitty, slips out
of the ant farm to visit the zoo, Alfred goes after him, digging all
the way down to "Z."
ISBN-13: 978-0-06-078760-8 (trade bdg.)
ISBN-10: 0-06-078760-0 (trade bdg.)
ISBN-13: 978-0-06-078761-5 (lib. bdg.)
ISBN-10: 0-06-078761-9 (lib. bdg.)
[1. Encyclopedias and dictionaries—Fiction. 2. Aardvark—Fiction.
3. Ants—Fiction. 4. Mother and child—Fiction.] I. Title.
PZ7.G29334Alf 2007 [E]—dc22 2006027874

First Edition 10 9 8 7 6 5 4 3 2 1

Greenwillow Books

A

a *n,* 1: the first letter of the English alphabet.

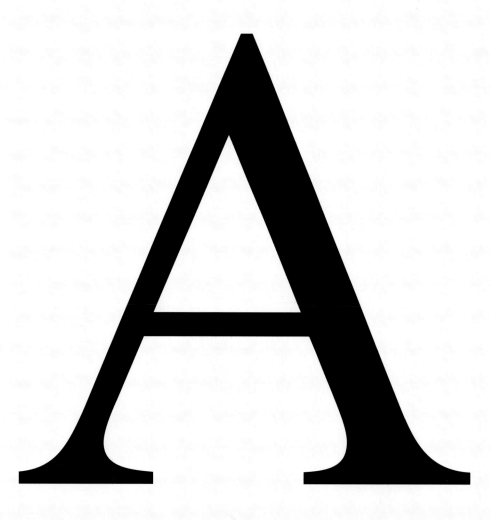

aard · vark *n,* : an African animal that is active at night. Aardvarks have long snouts and long, sticky tongues. They use their powerful front feet to dig burrows under the ground, where they live, and to rip open the nests of ants and termites, which they eat.

However, not *all* aardvarks eat ants.

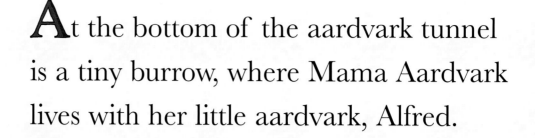

At the bottom of the aardvark tunnel is a tiny burrow, where Mama Aardvark lives with her little aardvark, Alfred.

Mama loves
her little aardvark,
and Alfred loves
his mama
and his pet ant,
Itty Bitty.
Alfred also loves
to dig.

One evening, Mama said, "Alfred, I'm taking this apple pie down to Mr. Alligator. I've left you a snack on the table. Remember, no digging while I'm gone."

"Okay, Mama," said Alfred.

"Little aardvark dear to me," Mama sang,

"I love you from A to . . ."

"Z!" Alfred shouted.

Alfred drank his milk
and ate his apple pie

and went to his room
to feed Itty Bitty.
But when he opened
the ant farm . . .

"Uh-oh!"

Dear Mama,
I have gone
to the zoo
to find Itty Bitty.
I will be home
soon.

Your son,
Alfred

Alfred scribbled
a note to his
mama,

slipped on
his goggles,

and started to dig . . .

and dig . . .

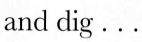

and dig,
down into
the dictionary.

He dug past . . .

B C D E

Q P O N

R S T

"Oh, no . . .

Itty Bitty's in trouble!"

Alfred jumped up,
stuck out his tongue,

and
rescued
Itty Bitty!

"Don't worry, Itty Bitty," said Alfred.
"I'll keep you safe."
But he could tell that the woodpecker
was still hungry.

SCRITCH SCRITCH SCRITCH...

What was that noise?

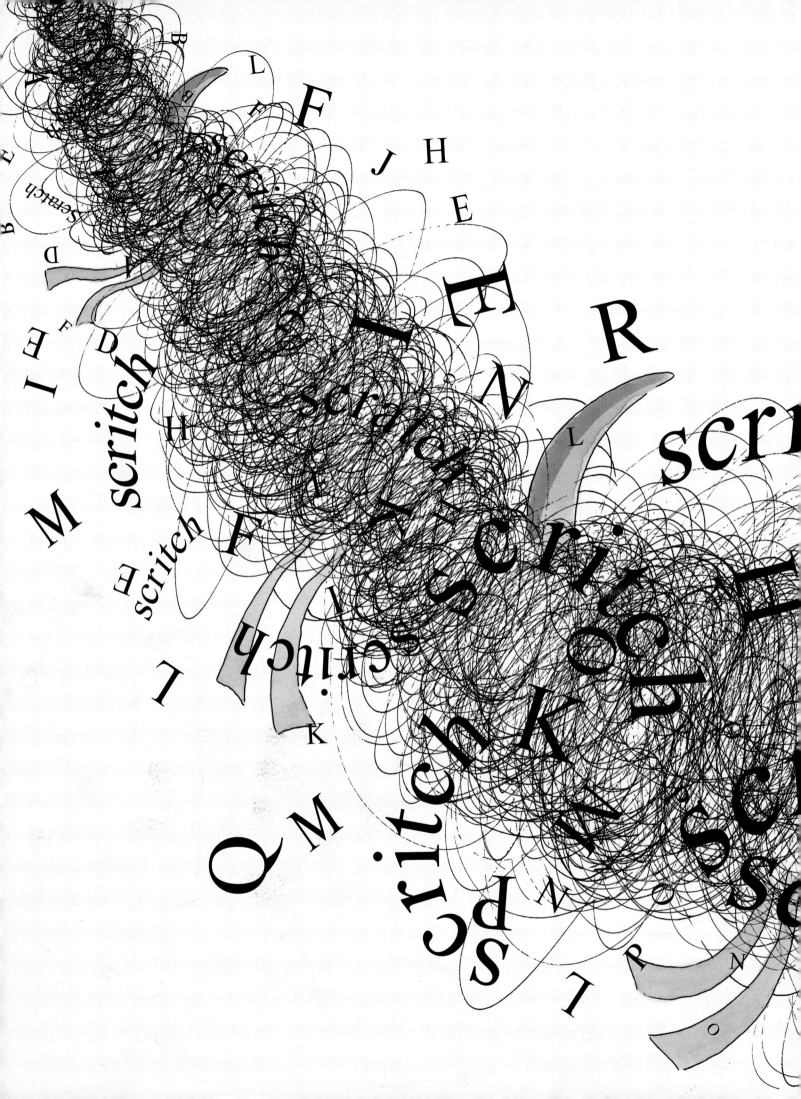

It was Mama!

Mama picked up Alfred
and gave him a kiss on his nose.

"I had to dig," said Alfred. "I had to find Itty Bitty."
"I know," said Mama.

"The woodpecker
was **sooo** big, Mama,"
said Alfred.

"He was very big," said Mama.
"And you were very brave."

E use me.
Bu now can
we go to
the zoo?

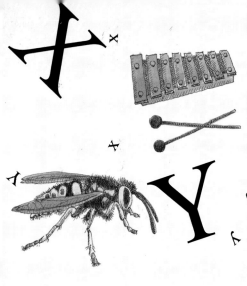

Mama and
Alfred
and
Itty Bitty
dug down
until they
reached
the zoo.

"That was fun, Mama!"
said Alfred.

"Yes, it was," Mama said,
"but now it is time to go home.
And I know just how to get there. Follow me!"

ZIG ZAG ZIG ZAG ZIG

ZAG ZIG ZAG ZIG ZAG ZIG ZAG ZIG

ZIG ZAG ZIG ZAG ZIG ZAG

ZIG ZAG ZIG ZAG ZIG ZAG ZIG

ZAG ZIG ZAG ZIG ZAG ZIG ZAG ZIG

ZIG ZAG ZIG ZAG ZIG ZAG ZIG ZAG ZIG ZAG

"Good evening, Mr. Zebra.
Can you give us
a ride home?" asked Mama.

"Of course, Mrs. Aardvark.
Welcome aboard!"

"Hold on tight, Alfred,"
Mama said.
"And Itty Bitty . . .
please get
in the cabin!"

Z

Mr. Zebra flew Alfred and
Itty Bitty and Mama
out of the dictionary . . .

and back to
the beginning
of the alphabet.

DICTIONARY

Home at last!

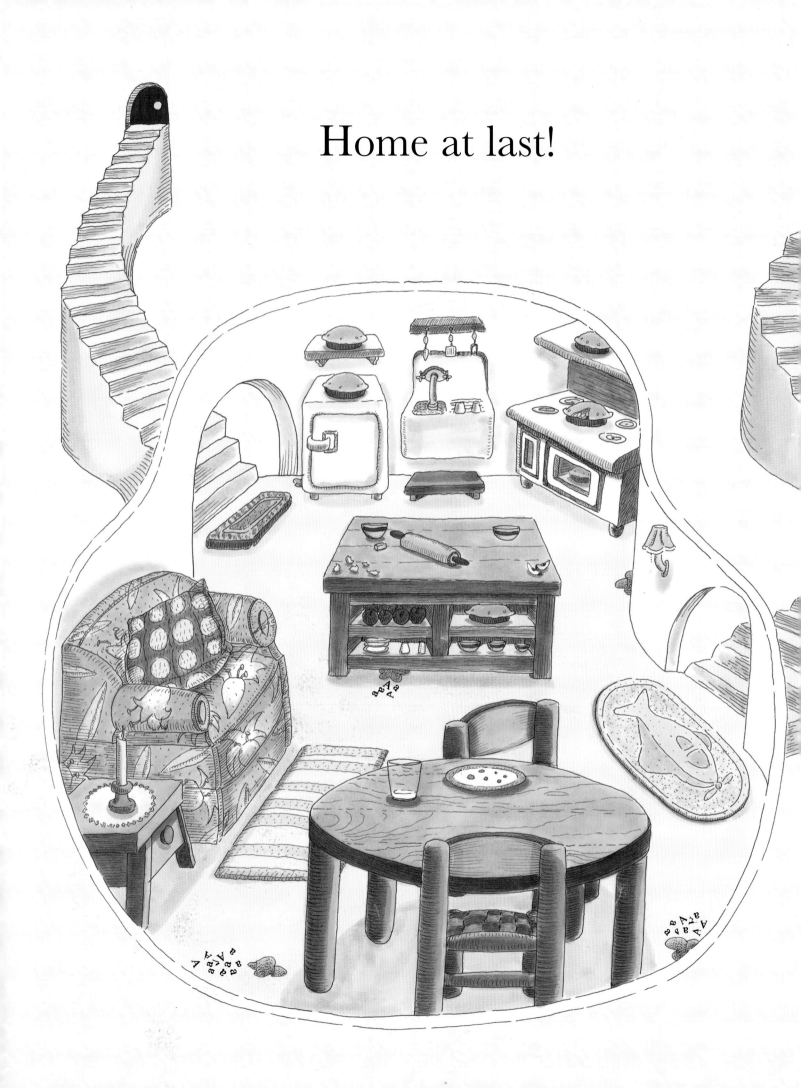

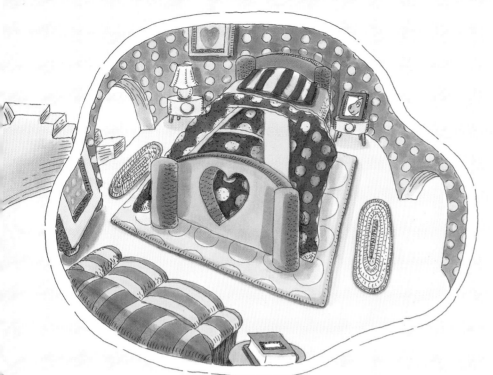

Mama tiptoed into
Alfred's bedroom.
"Good night,
Itty Bitty,"
she whispered.

"And sweet dreams,
my not-so-little one."

"Little aardvark
dear to me,
I love you
from A to . . ."